Two Little Dicky Birds

and

Two Little Puppy Dogs

Notes for adults

TADPOLES ACTION RHYMES provide support for newly independent readers and can also be used by adults for sharing with young children.

The language of action rhymes is often already familiar to an emergent reader and gives a highly supportive early reading experience.

The alternative rhymes extend this reading experience further, and encourage children to play with language and try out their own rhymes and actions.

If you are reading this book with a child, here are a few suggestions:

1. Make reading fun! Choose a time to read when you and the child are relaxed and have time to share the story.

2. Recite the rhyme together before you start reading. What might the alternative rhyme be about? Why might the child like it?

3. Encourage the child to reread the rhyme and do the actions, and to retell it in their own words, using the illustrations to remind them what has happened.

4. Point out together the rhyming words when the whole rhymes are repeated on pages 12 and 22 (developing phonological awareness will help with decoding) and encourage the child to make up their own new rhymes.

5. Give praise! Remember that small mistakes need not always be corrected.

First published in 2010 by
Franklin Watts
338 Euston Road
London NW1 3BH

Franklin Watts Australia
Level 17/207 Kent Street
Sydney, NSW 2000

Text (Two Little Puppy Dogs)
© Brian Moses 2010
Illustration © Barbara Vagnozzi 2010

The rights of Brian Moses to be identified
as the author of Two Little Puppy Dogs
and Barbara Vagnozzi as the illustrator of
this Work have been asserted in accordance
with the Copyright, Designs and Patents
Act, 1988.

ISBN 978 0 7496 9370 1 (hbk)
ISBN 978 0 7496 9376 3 (pbk)

Series Editor: Melanie Palmer
Series Advisors: Dr Hilary Minns
and Catherine Glavina
Series Designer: Peter Scoulding

Printed in China

Franklin Watts is a division of
Hachette Children's Books,
an Hachette Livre UK company.
www.hachettelivre.co.uk

Two Little Dicky Birds

Retold by Brian Moses
Illustrated by Barbara Vagnozzi

FRANKLIN WATTS
LONDON • SYDNEY

Barbara Vagnozzi

"I have a lot of animals, including a dog, three cats, four ducks and two rabbits – maybe that's why I like painting them!"

Two little dicky birds sitting on a wall,

one named Peter,

6

one named Paul.

Fly away, Peter,

8

fly away, Paul.

Come back, Peter,

10

come back, Paul!

Two Little Dicky Birds

Two little dicky birds

sitting on a wall,

one named Peter,

one named Paul.

Fly away, Peter,

fly away, Paul.

Come back, Peter,

come back, Paul!

Can you point to the
rhyming words?

Two Little Puppy Dogs

by Brian Moses
Illustrated by Barbara Vagnozzi

13

Brian Moses

"I do have a dog called Honey and when I told her she was in this book, her tail didn't stop wagging for ages!"

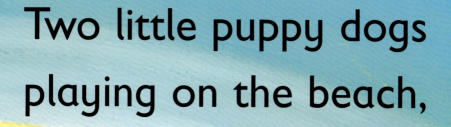

Two little puppy dogs playing on the beach,

15

one named Honey,

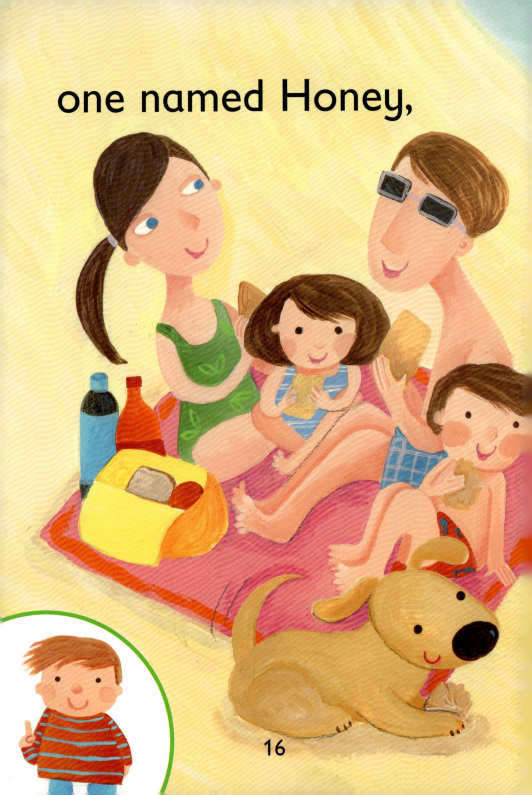

16

one named Peach.

Chase the ball, Honey!

Chase the ball, Peach!

Good dog, Honey,

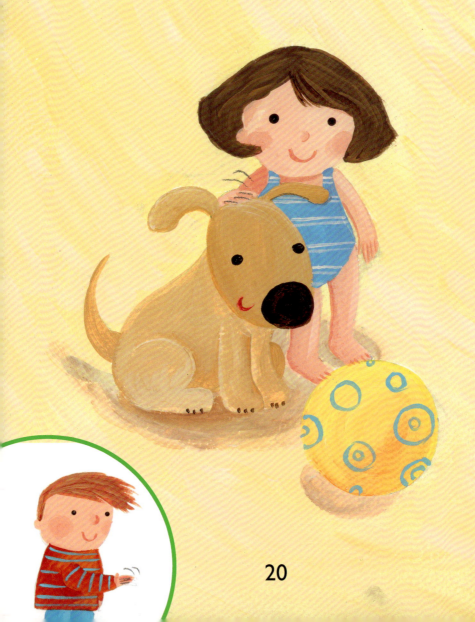

good dog, Peach.

Two Little Puppy Dogs

Two little puppy dogs

playing on the beach,

one named Honey,

one named Peach.

Chase the ball, Honey!

Chase the ball, Peach!

Good dog, Honey,

good dog, Peach.

Can you point to the
rhyming words?

Puzzle Time!

1.

2.

3.

Choose the right action
for the picture.

Answers

The correct action
is number 3.